A Rose for Abby

Donna Guthrie

Illustrated by
Dennis Hockerman

Abingdon Press / Nashville

A ROSE FOR ABBY

Library of Congress Cataloging-in-Publication Data

Guthrie, Donna.
    A rose for abby

    Summary: Abby, whose father preaches in a large urban church, sees a homeless old woman
    searching the trash cans nearby and is inspired to do something for the neighborhood's
    many street people.
    |1.Homeless persons—Fiction. 2. Churches—Fiction.
3. City and town life—Fiction| I. Title.
PZ7.G9834Ro 1988 |E| 88-10577
ISBN 0-687-36586-4 (pbk.: alk. paper)

PRINTED IN SINGAPORE

To my children, Carly and Colin

In the heart of a busy city on a street filled with rumbling trucks, honking taxis, and rushing cars lived a little girl named Abby. Her home was next to a large gray church where her father preached each Sunday.

On winter days after school Abby climbed the steps to the tiny library at the top of the church. It was her favorite place to play.

There she found the lost-and-found box with lost gloves and hats, forgotten sweaters, and an umbrella. Abby dressed up in the clothes and used the box as her doll's bed.

Late one afternoon, while playing by the window, Abby saw an old woman in ragged clothes digging in the trash cans. The woman pulled a cardboard box from the dumpster and put it over the heating vent in the sidewalk. She rubbed her hands together to get warm. Then the old woman climbed inside the box.

At supper that night, Abby told her father what she had seen. "Who is that woman?" asked Abby. "She looked so cold and lonely."

"That woman is one of the street people," said Abby's father.

"Why did she climb into that box?"

"She was trying to keep warm for the night. She doesn't have a home so she sleeps wherever she can."

"But who takes care of her?" asked Abby. "How does she eat?"

Abby's father shook his head. "I don't know," he said. "Sometimes the street people don't eat. Sometimes they go hungry."

"Could we give her something to eat?" asked Abby.

"I'd like to," said Abby's father. "But our church is poor. She's one of many, and we don't have enough money to feed all the street people."

When Abby went again to the little room at the top of the church, she watched for the old woman who slept in a box. Snow was falling against the windowpane.

Across the street Mrs. Snyder stared out her window too. Mrs. Snyder and her husband had lived on this street all their lives. The old couple sat each day looking out the window.

Farther down the street Abby could see Mr. Di Vito's large warehouse. The warehouse was filled with food. Trucks came each day to pick up meat, vegetables, and fruit.

Next door was Levine's Restaurant Supply Store. Mr. Levine sold dishes, pots, and pans. People from all over the city came to buy these things for their restaurants.

Down the snow-covered street came the old woman. She looked in each of the trash cans. There was nothing there. She rubbed her bare hands together. Abby could almost feel how cold she was. The old woman turned up her collar and walked on.

Abby sorted through the lost-and-found box. She found two gloves that were soft and warm. She drew a picture of a bright red flower on a brown paper bag. She put the gloves inside and put the bag into one of Mr. Di Vito's trash cans.

Abby was up in the little library waiting and watching from the window when the old woman came again. She stopped in front of Mr. Di Vito's warehouse. Carefully she opened the trash can and looked inside. The old woman took out the paper bag. She looked at the picture of the bright red flower. She opened the bag and took out the gloves. She put them on her bare hands, folded the bag, slipped it into the pocket of her coat, and walked on.

That night Abby took a hat from the lost-and-found box. She put it inside a brown paper bag and drew the same red flower on the outside. Early the next morning she put the bag in Mr. Di Vito's trash can.

Abby watched as the old woman made her way down the street, stopping at each trash can. She took the brown paper bag out of Mr. Di Vito's trash can and looked inside. The old woman looked up and down the street. She opened the bag and took out the hat. She put it on her head. She folded the bag, slipped it into the pocket of her coat, and walked on.

Abby saw Mr. and Mrs. Snyder sitting by their window.

She saw Mr. Di Vito checking the lock on the warehouse door.

She saw Mr. Levine arranging boxes of spoons, cups, and plates in the store window.

And standing in the doorway, waiting for the night, was the old woman.

Abby rushed down the steps into the church office where her father was taking off his black robe.

"Dad," she said, "do you know the box of lost things we've found in the church?"

"Yes," said her father, looking up from his work.

"I gave a pair of gloves and a hat to the old lady who lives on the street."

"That was a good idea," said her father.

"I think everybody on this street has something to give the old lady," said Abby.

"What do you mean?"

Abby told him her idea.

The next day Abby and her father visited Mr. Di Vito's market.

"What do you do with the vegetables that you don't sell?" asked Abby's father.

"We throw them away," answered Mr. Di Vito.

"Could we have them?" asked Abby. "We want to make soup for the people who live on the street."

"Of course," said Mr. Di Vito. "And I have some meat bones. They'll make a good broth."

Abby and her father thanked Mr. Di Vito. "We'll be back tomorrow for all that you can give."

They walked down the street to Levine's Restaurant Supply Store.

"Do you have any spoons, bowls, or cups?" Abby asked.

"Of course," said Mr. Levine. "How many do you need?"

"I'm not sure," said Abby. "Dad and I are making a soup, and we want to feed all the hungry people on our street."

"That's a lot of people," said Mr. Levine. He went to the back of the store and brought out three large boxes filled with mismatched spoons, chipped bowls, odd-size cups and glasses. "I can't sell these," said Mr. Levine. "You can use them to serve your soup."

On the way home, Abby and her father passed by Mr. and Mrs. Snyder's house. They waved from the window. Abby and her father stopped and rang the doorbell.

"Tomorrow we're making soup at our church," said Abby. "We want to serve it to all the hungry people on our street. Can you help us?"

"I'm a wonderful cook," said Mrs. Snyder.

"She is indeed," agreed her husband. "And I am strong so I can lift and carry. We both can help."

Early the next morning, Mr. Snyder, Abby, and her father set up four long tables in the church basement. They carried chairs from the church classrooms and put them around the tables.

Mrs. Snyder was working in the church kitchen. She placed a large pot of water on the stove. In the pot she put the meaty bones from Mr. Di Vito's market,

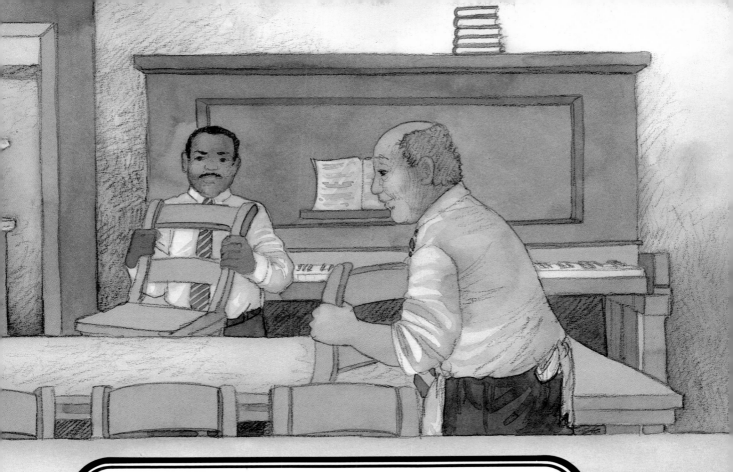

salt, pepper, and some spices from her own cupboard. Mr. Di Vito arrived with five tomatoes, four turnips, three yellow squash, and a sack of potatoes. Mrs. Snyder sliced and chopped the vegetables and added them to the pot. Soon the church basement was filled with the smell of a rich soup.

Mr. Snyder carried in the dishes. He put a spoon at every place. Abby drew a sign inviting everyone on the street to come for soup. On the sign she drew a bright red flower.

The street people began to come in the door. Mrs. Snyder gave a bowl of hot, steamy soup to everyone who came. Abby smiled at the old woman.

As people left, they thanked Abby, her father, and the Snyders for the wonderful meal. The old woman was the last to leave.

After everyone had left, Abby helped Mr. and Mrs. Snyder fold up the chairs and wash the tables. On the chair where the old woman had sat was Abby's brown paper bag.

Inside was a beautiful paper rose. Abby put the rose in her hair and slipped the brown paper bag into her pocket.